This book belongs to:

A Wonderful Wind

Disney's Out & About With Pooh
A Grow and Learn Library

Published by Advance Publishers
© 1996 Disney Enterprises, Inc.
Based on the Pooh stories by A. A. Milne © The Pooh Properties Trust.

Written by Ann Braybrooks
Illustrated by Arkadia Illustration Ltd.
Designed by Vickey Bolling
Produced by Bumpy Slide Books

ISBN:1-885222-67-X
10 9 8

One autumn night, the wind roared around Piglet's house, making the shutters bang and the branches thrash and creak.

As the wind moaned and Piglet dozed, he dreamed about another blustery day, when the wind had lifted him up into the sky like a kite. Luckily, Pooh had rescued him by holding onto a string that had come unraveled from Piglet's shirt.

The morning after his dream, when Pooh came to the door, Piglet peeked out and asked, "Is it still windy out? Because if it's windy *out*, I must stay *in*."

"It's all right, Piglet," said Pooh. "Last night's wind has

turned into a breeze. A breeze is much friendlier than a wind."

   Piglet stepped outside, and when he felt the warm, swirling air, he had to agree.

But just as Piglet was beginning to relax, the wind picked up again and whooshed through the woods, shaking the trees and sending the leaves tumbling. As Piglet's ears blew back, he pulled Pooh toward the house, crying, "Oh dear, oh dear, oh dear!"

Once they were inside, Piglet leaned against the door, hardly listening to Pooh, who said, "You never can tell with breezes. Sometimes they change their minds and become winds again."

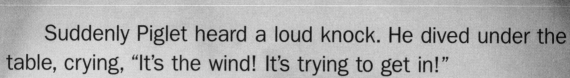

Suddenly Piglet heard a loud knock. He dived under the table, crying, "It's the wind! It's trying to get in!"

"I don't think so," said Pooh. "But I'll check, just in case." Pooh went to the door and shouted, "Go away, wind!"

"Open up!" replied the wind.

"Hmm," said Pooh, scratching his head. "The wind sounds a lot like Tigger. Maybe it's playing a trick on us."

Suddenly the door burst open, and in blew Roo and Tigger.

As they each held up a pinwheel, Roo said, "Come outside and watch them spin! They're so pretty when they turn!"

"What do you think, Piglet?" Pooh asked as Piglet crawled out from under the table.

"If I go outside," he asked Pooh, "you'll stay close to me, won't you?"

"Yes, Piglet," said Pooh. "Don't worry."

Outside in the wind, Piglet held Tigger's pinwheel and watched the spokes spin round and round.

"Now try mine," said Roo excitedly, handing his pinwheel to Piglet.

Piglet held out both pinwheels, feeling the wind rush around him, and suddenly found himself lifting off the ground.

"Pooh!" Piglet cried. "Help!"

Pooh quickly grabbed onto Piglet's feet and pulled him back to earth. Relieved, Piglet dropped the pinwheels and hugged his friend.

"Thank you, Pooh," he said breathlessly. "That was close!"

Just then Roo floated past them, holding both the pinwheels and squealing with delight.

"Look at me!" he called happily. "I'm flying!"

"Come back here!" Tigger called as he bounced up and took Roo's hand. "Your mother says you're too young to fly!"

Once Roo was safely back on the ground, Rabbit hurried by them, carrying a kite.

"Nice day for kite-flying!" called Pooh.

"And Piglet-flying and Roo-flying!" Tigger said to himself, giggling.

"Yes, it is!" Rabbit shouted. "It's too windy to garden, so I thought I'd fly this beauty instead. Would you like to come along?"

Pooh asked Piglet, "Do you want to go?"

"Oh, dear," said Piglet. "Do you?"

"It could be fun," said Pooh.

"I suppose," said Piglet, thinking. "All right. I'll go, as long as I can just watch."

So Piglet and the others followed Rabbit to a field, where they sat at the edge near some bushes and watched the wind snatch up Rabbit's kite and lift it into the sky.

As the friends sat together, Piglet noticed something swoop past him.

"Look, Pooh," said Piglet. "A spider."

They all watched as the spider, attached to a single

thread, blew from one bush to another. "The wind is helping it move," said Pooh. "That's another nice thing about wind."

"The spider could crawl," said Piglet.

"But flying is faster," said Pooh.

Just then they saw Owl overhead.

"Owl!" called Rabbit. "Look out for the kite!"

Owl swerved out of the way, caught a draft, and glided down to the grass. "Ah!" he said. "What a pleasant wind! It helps me fly, you know. All I have to do is find the right current, and in no time I get exactly where I want to go."

As Owl looked at his friends, a peculiar look came over his face.

"Someone's missing," he said. "Where's Eeyore?"

"I'm not sure," answered Pooh. "I haven't seen him today."

Owl was worried. "That was some storm last night," he said. "I think we'd better go over and see if Eeyore is all right."

So Rabbit reeled in his kite, and the friends hurried toward Eeyore's Gloomy Place.

There they found Eeyore and Christopher Robin.
"Amazing!" observed Owl. "All that wind, and you still have a house. Weren't you worried?"
"Yes," Eeyore said. "But the wind was making a nice,

sad sort of tune. I hummed along, and before I knew it, the storm was over. It was almost fun."

"Well," announced Christopher Robin, "I know another way to have fun on a windy day. Come with me!"

The friends followed Christopher Robin to a small lake, where an old but sturdy sailboat was tied to a dock.

"Get in, everyone!" invited Christopher Robin.

As the friends clambered into the sailboat, Owl said, "A jaunt around the lake sounds splendid, but I'm off to help Kanga with some baking. Why don't you join me there for tea later? I'm sure she won't mind."

The friends hopped aboard. Christopher Robin steered the boat so the wind could fill the sail. In no time, the sailboat was gliding across the water.

Pooh turned to Piglet and asked, "Is it too breezy for you?"

"I'm fine," said Piglet. "As long as I hold on tight, I probably won't fly away."

Pooh moved closer and put his arm around his friend.

"I won't let you go," he said reassuringly.

For a while the wind gusted gustily, sending the boat around the lake in lovely loops. But when the wind got tired of pushing, the boat drifted to the middle of the lake, and Christopher Robin said, "Oh, my!"

Piglet lifted his head. "What happened?" he asked.

"Nothing much," said Pooh. "There isn't any wind, so we're stuck."

"Stuck?" said Piglet.

"Until more wind comes," said Christopher Robin.

As the friends waited, Piglet gazed around the lake and tried not to worry. For the first time, he wished the wind would return, and when he felt something tug at his ears, he sat up straight in his seat.

"It's here!" Piglet squeaked.

Quickly, while the wind puffed up the sail, Christopher Robin brought the boat back to the dock, and the friends hopped off.

After Christopher Robin tied up the boat, they all headed toward Kanga and Roo's house.

Along the way, Tigger sniffed and said, "I smell a skunk."

Pooh pointed up the path. "There it is," he said. "We're downwind!"

As they stared, the skunk saw them and shyly turned off the path.

A while later, Tigger said, "Now what do I smell?"

"Haycorn pie!" said Piglet.

"No!" cried Roo. "Chocolate!"

Pooh pointed his nose in the air. "Yum," he said, closing his eyes and breathing deeply. "I smell honey!"

"Come and get it!" Kanga called, her voice carrying on the wind. "It's time for tea!"

"What do you think of the wind now?" Pooh asked Piglet.

"It makes pinwheels spin," exclaimed Tigger.

"And kites fly," added Rabbit.

"And owls glide," offered Owl.

"And boats sail," noted Christopher Robin.

"The wind can also whistle a tune," Eeyore said.
"And carry smells from here to there!" remembered Roo.
Piglet sat up bravely in his chair. "I think," he said, "we should open a window and enjoy the lovely afternoon breeze!"